A book made for:

_____

Made by:

DOG

_____

PICTURE BOOK BY DOG

MICHAEL RELTH

Little, Brown and Company
New York Boston

Hello,
my name is
DOG,

and I
made you
this book.

I'd like to share my story.
Won't you have
a look?

I was lost
before we met.
On my own,
I roamed
around—

hungry, wet, and
searching for the home
I'd never found.

Some caring people picked me up and took me somewhere dry. They washed and groomed me, gave me food...

...but sometimes I'd still cry. Even though the place was full, I often felt alone.

I dreamed I had a special friend.
I wished I had a home.

The day you opened up my cage,
I first thought, "Could
it be...?"

Of all the dogs
to choose from,

why on earth
did you
pick me?

You brought me home and gave me many toys, a leash, a bed...

three tennis balls, a collar,
and a bowl to keep me fed.

First I had to find out
what to chew
and NOT to chew.

And then I learned
the hard way where to
poo and **NOT** to poo!

Back then, you were my teacher.
You taught me GOOD

We snuggled,
played, explored
the world....

Now you're the friend
I'd never had.

I look forward to the times ahead, when you'll grow **BIG** one day.

I'll be an old and happy dog
with fur that's turning gray.

...that the reason
life has been
so sweet...

...is
because
we are
family.

NOTE FROM DOG:
I know LOTS of dogs who could use a home and a good friend like YOU!